ANIMAL TEAMWORK

WOLVES WORK TOGETHER

MIKE SCOUT

PowerKiDS press.
New York

Published in 2018 by The Rosen Publishing Group, Inc.
29 East 21st Street, New York, NY 10010

First Edition

Editor: Melissa Raé Shofner
Book Design: Michael J. Flynn

Photo Credits: Cover Diane Shapiro/Photolibrary/Getty Images; p. 4 Millard H Sharp/Science Source/Getty Images; p. 5 Nadezda Murmakova/Shutterstock.com; p. 6 Sbolotova/Shutterstock.com; p. 7 Dennis W Donohue/Shutterstock.com; p. 9 (map) ekler/Shutterstock.com; pp. 9 (wolf), 22 David Osborn/Shutterstock.com; pp. 10–11 Panoramic Images/Getty Images; p. 13 Geoffrey Kuchera/Shutterstock.com; p. 15 Nagel Photography/Shutterstock.com; p. 17 Bildagentur Zoonar GmbH/Shutterstock.com; p. 19 Lori Labrecque/Shutterstock.com; p. 21 Arto Hakola/Shutterstock.com.

Cataloging-in-Publication Data

Names: Scout, Mike.
Title: Wolves work together / Mike Scout.
Description: New York : PowerKids Press, 2018. | Series: Animal teamwork | Includes index.
Identifiers: ISBN 9781508155492 (pbk.) | ISBN 9781508155430 (library bound) | ISBN 9781508155317 (6 pack)
Subjects: LCSH: Wolves–Juvenile literature. | Wolves–Behavior–Juvenile literature.
Classification: LCC QL737.C22 S36 2018 | DDC 599.773–dc23

Manufactured in the United States of America

CPSIA Compliance Information: Batch #BS17PK: For Further Information contact Rosen Publishing, New York, New York at 1-800-237-9932

CONTENTS

WOLVES OF THE WORLD

Wolves are awesome animals. They're beautiful and frightening at the same time. The most widespread species, or kind, of wolf is the gray wolf. Scientists can't agree on exactly how many subspecies there are. However, they do agree that wolves of all kinds are masters of teamwork.

This book focuses on gray wolves and how they work together to raise their pups, hunt large animals, and keep their pack safe. Gray wolves use teamwork each day to survive in the wild.

RED WOLF

CRITTER COOPERATION

Red wolves are uncommon. They're only found in a small area of North Carolina, and there are fewer than 100 in the wild.

Eurasian wolves are a type of gray wolf. They're found throughout Europe and Asia.

THE GRAY WOLF

Gray wolves are **mammals**. They may be about 4.5 to 6.5 feet (1.4 to 2 m) long, including their tail. They can weigh 60 to 135 pounds (27.2 to 61.2 kg). Female wolves are usually smaller than males.

CRITTER COOPERATION

Wolves are the largest members of the dog family. They look a lot like some of the types of dogs we keep as pets. Don't be fooled, though—wolves are wild!

It may surprise you to learn that not all gray wolves are gray. These animals may be many different colors, including gray, black, white, and brown. The color of their fur often depends on where they live. Wolves living in Arctic areas, for example, often have white fur.

Wolves have strong legs, warm fur, pointed ears, and sharp teeth.

WHERE DO WOLVES LIVE?

Gray wolves live throughout Canada and Alaska, in parts of Europe and Asia, and in other small areas of the United States. They can live in many **habitats**, including mountains, forests, deserts, plains, and Arctic areas. Wolves try to find areas with lots of **prey**, and they avoid living near people whenever possible.

A group of wolves is called a pack. Each wolf pack has its own territory. Depending on where a pack lives, its territory may be 1,000 square miles (2,590 km sq) or larger!

CRITTER COOPERATION

Wolves usually live for about eight years in the wild, although some may live to be several years older. Some wolves remain with the same pack for their whole life.

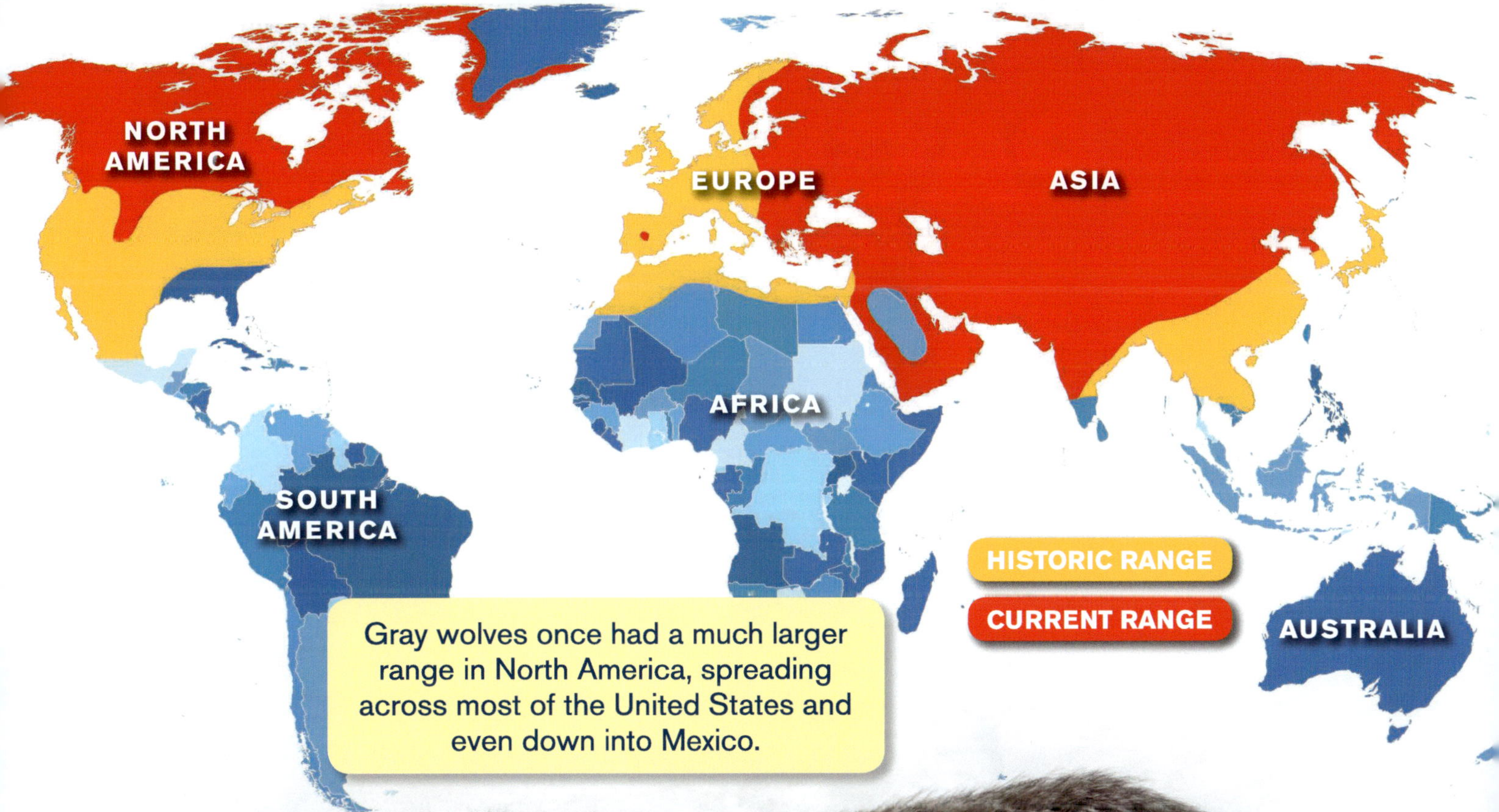

Gray wolves once had a much larger range in North America, spreading across most of the United States and even down into Mexico.

PACK LIFE

A pack is a close-knit family of wolves. There are usually about 8 to 12 wolves in a pack. Very large packs may have more than 30 members. A male and female, called alphas, lead each pack. Members of a pack include the alphas and their offspring, or young, of different ages.

Wolves are social animals. Pack members form close bonds with each other.

Wolf packs are **hierarchal** societies. Each member has a rank and an important role in the pack. The alphas are the highest-ranking members. They're dominant, or in charge. The lowest-ranking member is called the omega.

CRITTER COOPERATION

The hierarchy of a pack creates strong bonds between members because they all must work together.

RAISING WOLF PUPS

The alpha wolves within a pack form a life-long bond and are the only pack members that **mate**. When a female wolf is ready to have babies, she finds or digs a den. Newborn pups stay in the den for several weeks.

All members of a wolf pack help to care for pups. They take turns **regurgitating** food for them to eat. When the pups are about six weeks old, pack members start to bring them meat. When they're about 10 months old, pups begin to hunt with the pack.

CRITTER COOPERATION

Pups leave the den and begin to play fight a few weeks after they're born. How they act around each other and other pack members at this time helps decide their rank in the pack.

Wolf pups grow fast. They're almost as big as the adults by the time they're six months old!

HOWLS AND GROWLS

Wolves work together so well because they **communicate** a lot. They howl to let other pack members know where they are and when they should gather for a hunt. Wolves also bark, growl, cry, and make many other noises.

Wolves also communicate using body language. You can often figure out a wolf's rank by the way it walks up to or touches another wolf. Lower-ranking wolves will crawl and roll over in front of higher-ranking wolves.

CRITTER COOPERATION

Just as all people have different fingerprints, all wolves have different howls. Scientists can tell two wolves apart just by listening to them howl. Other wolves can do this, too!

Wolves don't actually howl at the moon. It just seems that way because they howl more when it's lighter at night, which is often the case when there's a full moon.

BUILT FOR THE WILD

Wolves have several **adaptations** that help them work together to survive in the wild. They have great hearing and can hear other wolves as far as 10 miles (16.1 km) away! They also have an excellent sense of smell and can pick up a scent from as far as 1.75 miles (2.8 km) away.

Wolves have thick fur to keep them warm. Pack members groom, or clean, each other by licking and chewing on each other's coats. They'll also groom injured, or hurt, wolves to comfort them.

CRITTER COOPERATION

Wolves have very large paws. This helps them walk and run on top of soft snow without sinking.

Wolves' paws have adapted to let them travel over many surfaces, including rocks and snow, with ease. Wolves can keep moving quickly, and they don't easily get tired.

ON THE HUNT

Gray wolves are carnivores, which means they eat meat. They're one of the few animals on Earth that can hunt prey larger than themselves, such as moose, bison, and elk. They do this by using teamwork!

The alphas will often track prey and the pack will follow them. Wolves spend a lot of time moving around their territory searching for food. Sometimes they travel more than 50 miles (80.5 km) a day. Wolves work together to creep up on and bring down a large kill.

CRITTER COOPERATION

Wolves are fast! They can run for about 20 minutes at speeds up to 38 miles (61.2 km) an hour. Packs run together while hunting.

Wolves can eat up to 20 pounds (9.1 kg) of meat at a time. They don't make large kills every day, though. They'll eat smaller animals when large prey is hard to find.

PROTECTING THE PACK

Gray wolves are apex predators. This means they're at the top of the food chain in their habitat and have few predators. Sometimes wolves **compete** with other animals, such as bears or coyotes, for food. These animals usually won't attack wolves because they don't want to fight a whole pack. However, they may attack a wolf if it's alone.

The territory of one wolf pack sometimes overlaps with that of another pack. Packs usually avoid each other, but sometimes packs will fight.

CRITTER COOPERATION

Wolves' bodies produce scents that are used to mark their territory and let other wolves know that an area has been claimed.

Wolves are more open to attack when they're alone. Pack members hunt and eat together to stay safe.

WOLVES AND PEOPLE

Wolves were once seen as little more than a danger to people and livestock. In the 1930s, wolves were hunted to near **extinction** in the United States. Today, we understand that wolves play an important role in the **ecosystem**. They keep the populations of other animals, such as deer, under control.

Conservation efforts have helped wolves make a comeback in many areas. Attacks on livestock, pets, and people sometimes do happen, but we've come a long way in learning how to live alongside wolves.

GLOSSARY

adaptation: A change in a living thing that helps it live better in its habitat.

communicate: To share ideas and feelings through sounds and motions.

compete: To try to get something that another animal wants.

conservation: Efforts to care for the natural world.

ecosystem: A natural community of living and nonliving things.

extinction: The state of no longer existing.

habitat: The natural home for plants, animals, and other living things.

hierarchal: Arranged by rank or class.

mammal: Any warm-blooded animal whose babies drink milk and whose body is covered with hair or fur.

mate: To come together to make babies.

prey: An animal hunted by other animals for food.

regurgitate: The act of throwing up partially eaten food.

INDEX

WEBSITES

Due to the changing nature of Internet links, PowerKids Press has developed an online list of websites related to the subject of this book. This site is updated regularly. Please use this link to access the list: www.powerkidslinks.com/atw/wolv